Mortimer's Christmas Manger

Karma Wilson ★ Jane Chapman

Margaret K. McElderry Books

New York   London   Toronto   Sydney

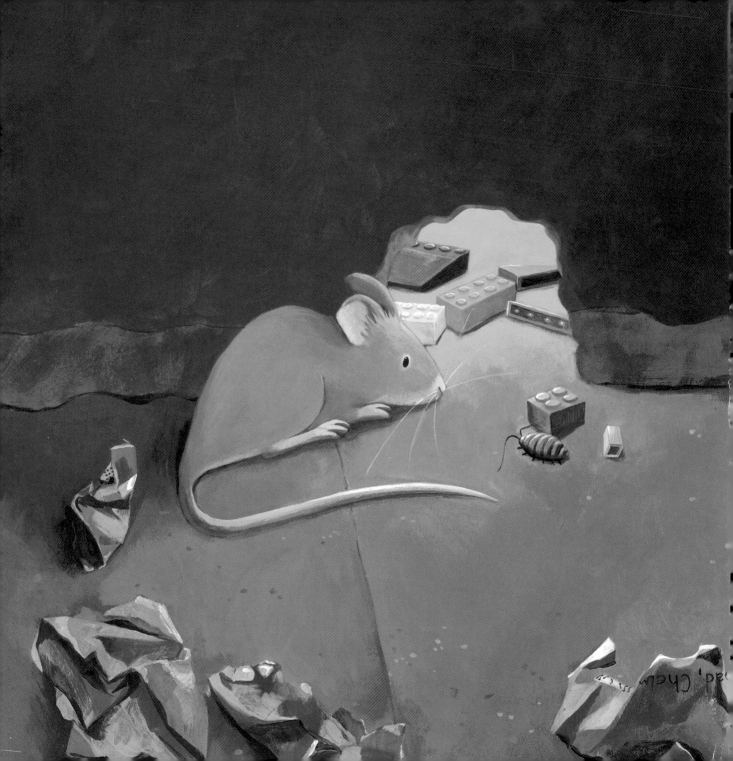

To Jesus, who cares for all,
from the mightiest king to the tiniest mouse. Thank you.
—K. W.

To Tiphanie, Barnaby, Joshua, and John
—J. C.

Margaret K. McElderry Books
An imprint of Simon & Schuster Children's Publishing Division
1230 Avenue of the Americas, New York, New York 10020
Text copyright © 2005 by Karma Wilson
Illustrations copyright © 2005 by Jane Chapman
This edition copyright © 2007
All rights reserved, including the right of reproduction in whole or in part in any form.
Book design by Sonia Chaghatzbanian
The text for this book is set in Bembo.
The illustrations for this book are rendered in acrylic paint.
Manufactured in China
6 8 10 9 7
CIP data for this book is available from the Library of Congress.
ISBN-13: 978-1-4169-5049-3 ★ ISBN-10: 1-4169-5049-4
0711 SCP

In a big house
lived a wee mouse
named Mortimer.
He dwelled
in a dark hole
under the stairs.

Nobody ever noticed little Mortimer.
And Mortimer liked it that way.
But he didn't like his hole.
"Too cold. Too cramped. Too creepy,"
squeaked Mortimer.

Each day he snuck out
and crept about looking
for crumbs and tidbits.
One day . . .

Mortimer spied something new. What he spied was wonderful!

He saw a huge tree covered
with twinkling lights. Nestled
on top was a bright, shining star.
But something even
better than the tree itself
sat next to it on a table.
Mortimer sighed with delight.
"A house just my size!"

But the house
was so high
and Mortimer
was so low.

"I'll climb up the tree,"
said Mortimer.
It made a perfect ladder . . .
for a mouse.

Up, up, up Mortimer climbed. Down, down, down ornaments crashed.

Finally he reached the table.
"Perfect," said Mortimer. "Not cold. Not
cramped. Not creepy. Cozy! But—who are you?"

Mortimer had never seen people so small.
Almost as small as himself. He had never seen
such strange animals, either.

Tap . . . tap . . . tap . . .
Mortimer
knocked,
but no one
answered.

Tap . . . tap . . . tap . . .
No one moved an inch.

"I see," Mortimer
squeaked. "You
aren't real!
Only statues!"

And so, Mortimer lugged . . . and Mortimer tugged.
One by one he dragged the statues out.

When he reached the
smallest statue, he saw it
was . . . a baby. A baby
in a wooden bed just
Mortimer's size.

"There's no room for
you here," Mortimer said.
"Out you go."

Then into bed crawled Mortimer.
He fell fast asleep in the soft, warm hay.

The next day, as Mortimer crept about,
he found good things to eat.
Cookie crumbs, fruitcake morsels,
and spicy peppermint candy.

But when Mortimer
scampered back up to his
new home, the statues
were set up again.

"No,
no,
no!"
squeaked Mortimer.
"This won't do.
There's no room
for me!"

And so . . .

Mortimer lugged . . .

and Mortimer tugged . . .

until all the statues were out.
"And stay out!" he said.

Then into bed crawled Mortimer.
He fell fast asleep
in the soft, warm hay.

But each day, while Mortimer scurried about,
the statues were set up again.

And Mortimer
always lugged
and tugged them
back out.

Then one day . . .

Mortimer set out and saw the big people gathered around the tree. He couldn't go out there, so he hid among the statues. A man started talking.

Mortimer listened. And what he heard was wonderful!

*"Since it is Christmas Eve, I shall
tell the Christmas story,"*
said the man. *"A long time ago
in a little town called Bethlehem . . ."*

Mortimer heard about people
named Joseph and Mary and a
bright, shining star.
He heard about shepherds
watching their flocks by night
and traveling wise men.
The man continued . . .

"And there was no room for them in the inn."

Then Mortimer heard about a baby.
A baby who was born in a stable and had no real bed but slept in a wooden manger. A baby born to save the world!

"And His name shall be called Jesus," said the man.

Mortimer looked at the bright, shining star on the tree. He looked at his new home and his new bed. He looked at the statues.

Last of all, he looked at the baby.
"I see . . . ," sighed Mortimer.
"You aren't just any statue.
You are a statue of Jesus."

Mortimer sniffed.
Mortimer snuffled.
A tear rolled down his furry cheek.
"There was no room for you in the inn.
But I know where there is room," he said.

And so . . .

Mortimer lugged . . .
and Mortimer tugged.
Soon he dragged all
the statues back to
where they belonged.

Last of all, he laid the baby in the manger.
"This belongs to you," he said.
Mortimer smiled.
"You look warm and cozy now."

There was no place for Mortimer
to go except back to the cold,
cramped, creepy hole.

As Mortimer scuttled down the tree,
he said a prayer: "Jesus, you were
born to save the world. Perhaps you
could also bring me a home?"

And then Mortimer
spied something new.
What he spied was wonderful!
Mortimer sighed with delight.
"A house just my size."
There were no statues in sight.
And so . . .

Mortimer moved right in.
"Thank you, Jesus," said Mortimer.
"You've made room for me, too."